To Adam, our sweetheart,
with love, hugs and kisses from
Mum, Dad, Harry, Robbie and Molly.

Adam is an angel and lives on a cloud
and makes his Mummy and Daddy so proud.
With long golden hair you just could not miss,
he always has time for a hug and a kiss.
The message he sends from his cloud every day,
is to spend more time with each other and play.
The most important thing in life is this,
show your love for your family with a hug and a kiss.

Written by Benji Bennett.
benji@adamscloud.com

Illustrations by Roxanne Burchartz.
Roxanneburchartz@gmail.com

Designed by Bold.
www.reallybold.com

This 2014 first edition printed in Ireland by Watermans Printers.
www.watermansprinters.ie

ISBN 978-1-906818-09-8

Published by

An imprint of Adam's Printing Press Publishing.

Adam's Cloud is dedicated to spreading Adam's message of the importance of love, laughter and play within the family
and will make a donation from the proceeds of all books published under its imprint to children's charities.

Adam's Cloud, PO Box 11379, Blackrock, Co. Dublin, Ireland.
Email: info@adamscloud.com   Web: www.adamscloud.com   Tel: +353 1 283 3620

2% of the proceeds from the sale of this book will go to

IRELAND'S CHILDREN'S HOSPICE

Inspired by the memory of their two beautiful daughters, Laura and Lynn, Brendan and Jane McKenna established LauraLynn, Ireland's Children's Hospice which
provides home-support, respite and palliative care to children with life-limiting conditions. The LauraLynn House is not a sad place but a place for living and a
place of fun, laughter, enjoyment, love and support. While we cannot change a child's diagnosis, we can change the quality of a child's life and their families.
LauraLynn receive no state funding and rely solely on fund raising, and very much appreciate the wonderful support from Adam and his friends.
To support, please contact fundraising@lauralynn.ie or see our website www.lauralynn.ie

"Hey everybody!" Adam said, "let's play dress up in our room.
Molly, you can be the princess bride and Robbie, you're the groom.
Harry you can be our mighty brave and noble knight
And I can be the wizard with a magic wand of light."

Just as they started playing, Fluff flew up to their window
"Adam," he said, "we need your help, quick we have to go."
"What is it?" Adam said, as he hopped up on Fluff's back
"It's the land of hugs and kisses,
the Wicked Witch is back."

"She took the hugs and kisses from the hugs and kisses Fairy
And she's too afraid to get them back 'coz the Witch is mean and scary."
"Oh dear!" cried Adam "We better hurry, but how will we get there?"
Fluff replied, "With some magic from a rainbow and a lock of fairy hair."

"Easy Peasy!"

Fluff quickly zoomed into the sky at the speed of light
To catch the magic rainbow and the fairies out that night.
Just then, right out of nowhere, a secret path was cleared
When the fairies cast their magic spell and a rainbow bridge appeared.

**"Hold on tight!"** Adam screamed, "hold on with all your might.
This will probably be our most important ever flight."
When they arrived in Fairyland, something strange had happened.
All their dress up clothes became the best ones ever fashioned.

"Hey Robbie, Robbie look!" cried Molly, "I'm like a real princess."
"I know," said Robbie, "You look so nice and what a lovely dress."

# "Whoa! We look so cool,"

said Adam, "But quick we better hurry
And find the Fairy Queen because
We don't want her to worry."

Off they set along a trail to find the Fairy Queen
And very soon they found the biggest castle ever seen.
"Hey Robbie," Molly giggled "I'm glad we're so well dressed
If we're going to meet the Fairy Queen we want to look our best."

"Shush! Be very quiet,"

whispered Adam, "or we'll scare the Queen away
Without her hugs and kisses she could be shy and run away."
"Oh! Poor little hugs and kisses Fairy," Molly said.
"Come on Molly," Harry said, "the door is up ahead."

They reached the fairy castle door and softly in they went
And found the worried Fairy Queen in her magic fairy tent.
"Oh! Adam," said the Fairy Queen, "the world will never be the same
If children don't get a hug or kiss and the Witch is all to blame.

"We can help," said Robbie, "can't we? We have a Wizard and a Knight.
Surely we are brave enough to fight the Witch tonight."
"You are," replied the Fairy Queen, "but wear this by your chest
It holds some magic fairy dust to protect you on your quest."

She gave them all a magic stone that felt as cold as snow.
"Now, there's one last thing," she said, "that you should know before you go.
When you are safe your wand will glow magnificently bright
But beware, when you are in danger it will be dim and hardly light."

"Hurry! Hurry! Chicken Curry! Quick we have to go,"
Giggled Adam, as he held his magic wand that brightly glowed.
Fluff bravely flew the fearless bunch of wizards, wands and knights
To the Wicked Witches castle that soon was in their sights.

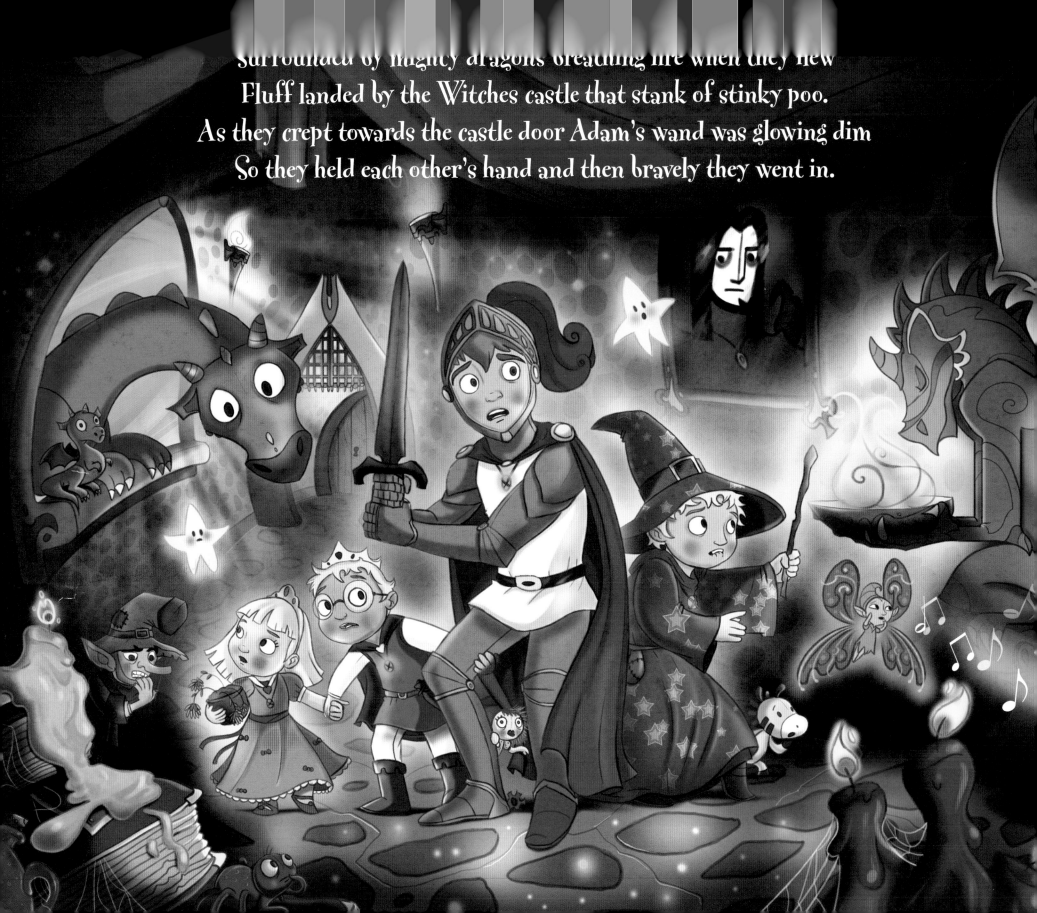

surrounded by mighty dragons breathing fire when they flew
Fluff landed by the Witches castle that stank of stinky poo.
As they crept towards the castle door Adam's wand was glowing dim
So they held each other's hand and then bravely they went in.

They snuck around and soon they found the witch and witchy broom
Doing a jig and singing a song and dancing around the room.

"Ha Ha! He He!
I have them all; I have them all I say
No more hugs and kisses
for the fairy's kids today."

"**She's so mean,**" Adam thought, "taking all the hugs and kisses."
Then Adam noticed something strange he thought was quite suspicious.
A picture lay upon the wall of a happy little baby
Then Adam wondered if the Witch was just a sad old lady.

Who never had a hug or kiss when she was just a kid
And when her friends came out to play she ran away and hid.
The more that Adam thought of this he began to realise
That the Wicked Witch, just may be, a nice one in disguise.

"I have it guys!" Adam said, "I know what we should do.
But if my plan is going to work you have to help me too."
Everybody gathered round and agreed upon a plan
And on the count of 3 their clever plan began.

They all jumped on the Wicked Witch and pinned her to the ground
and smothered her with hugs and kisses until she nearly drowned.
Then, all of a sudden, in a magic flash of light
The Wicked Witch's evil cloak was changed from black to white.

**"Yahooooo! We did it,"** everyone exclaimed,
"With all our hugs and kisses the Wicked Witch has changed"
Fluff flew them back to the magic Fairy Kingdom quickly
And Adam told the story of their adventure and their victory.

"Oh Fairy Queen we were so scared of the evil Wicked Witch
But I knew a hug and kiss would make the good and bad Witch switch."
"Adam," said the Fairy Queen, "you saved all of Fairyland."
"You're welcome." Adam said, and then he kissed the Fairy's hand.

Then with a flash of lightning, the Rainbow reappeared
And with the magic of the Fairies the way back home was cleared.
"It's time to go." said Adam, "Our important job is done,
But visiting your kingdom was the
# Very best of fun."

Then Fluff zoomed over the rainbow bridge to bring them all back home
Always to be kept safe by their magic fairy stone.
"That was some adventure Adam," Harry yawned and said,
And with that they all lay down and slept safely in their beds.

It's time to sleep my baby belle,
Safely under a fairy spell.
Filled with all my love, hugs and kisses,
Sprinkled with magical wonderful wishes.